For Paul, my salty, blue-eyed man of the sea.

Text and illustrations copyright © Susan Steggall 2010
The right of Susan Steggall to be identified as the author and illustrator of this work has been asserted by her
in accordance with the Copyright, Designs and Patents Act, 1988 (United Kingdom).

First published in Great Britain in 2010 and in the USA in 2011 by
Frances Lincoln Children's Books, 4 Torriano Mews,
Torriano Avenue, London NW5 2RZ
www.franceslincoln.com

A catalogue record for this book is available from the British Library.

ISBN 978-1-84780-074-9

Illustrated with collages of torn papers

Set in Today

Printed in Dongguan, Guangdong, China by Toppan Leefung in May 2010

1 3 5 7 9 8 6 4 2

BUSY BOATS

Susan Steggall

F

FRANCES LINCOLN
CHILDREN'S BOOKS

Judder, judder, judder,
as the engines shudder,
the fishermen are heading out to sea.

The cranes have started loading,

the cargo boats are groaning,

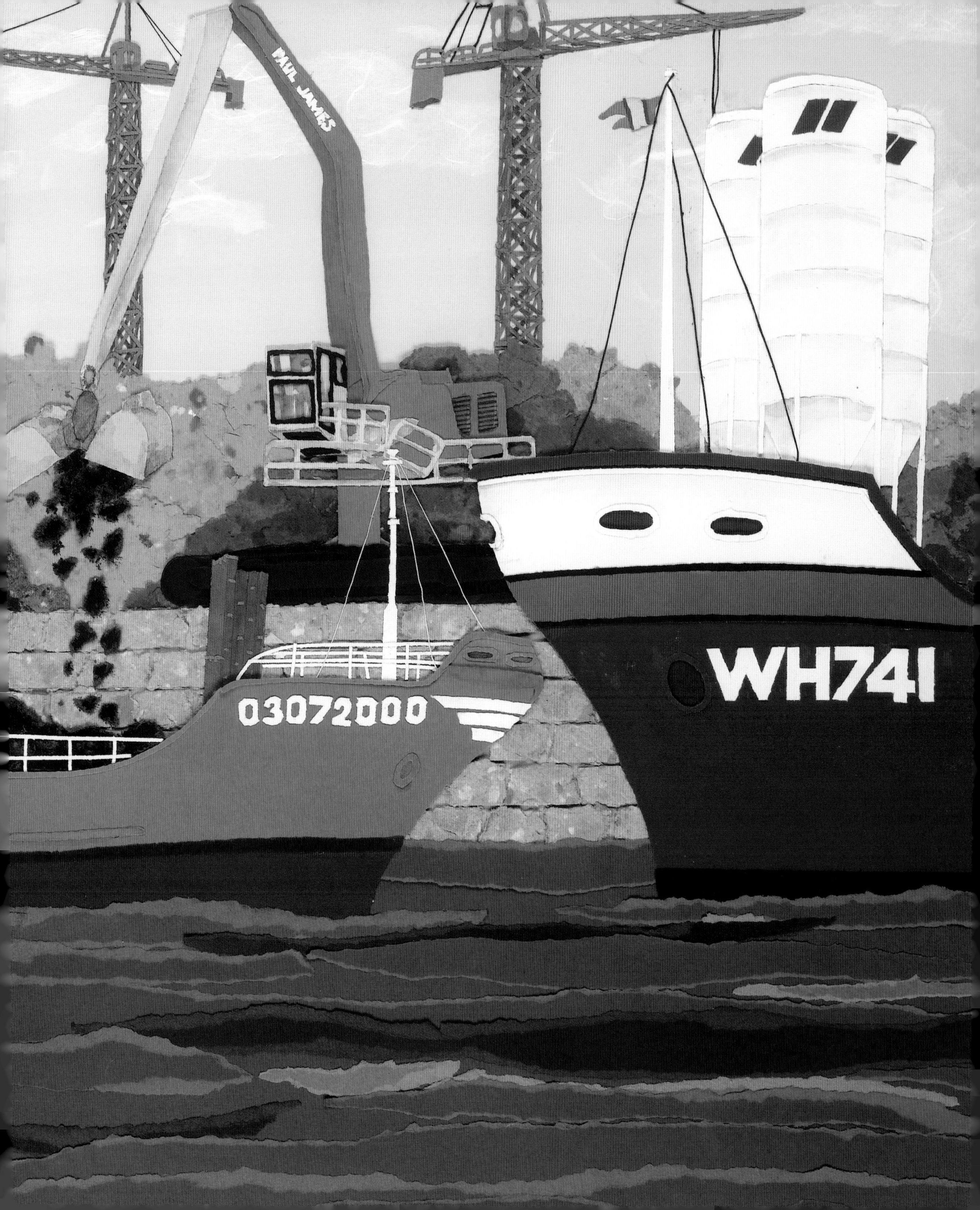
PAUL JAMES
03072000
WH741

and the tourist boats are filling up,
it's nearly time to go.

The motor boats are chugging,

the tug boats soon come tugging,

and the ferry boats are ferrying, to and fro.

The rescue boats go racing by,

the seagulls screech and squawk and cry,

and the rowing boats are bobbing, high and low.

Judder, judder, judder, as the engines shudder,

the fishermen are coming home to tea.